THIS

READ with ME ™

BOOK
BELONGS TO

Danielle

Library of Congress Cataloging in Publication Data

Perle, Ruth Lerner.
    Snow White and the seven dwarfs, with Benjy
and Bubbles.

    (Read With Me series)
    SUMMARY: A rhymed retelling of the classic
tale with Benjy the bunny and Bubbles the cat
clarifying values as the story unfolds.
    [1. Stories in rhyme. 2. Fairy tales.
3. Folklore—Germany] I. Razzi, James.
II. Title. III. Series.
PZ8.3.P423Sn   398.2   [E]   77-17680
    ISBN 0-03-040231-X

Snow White and the Seven Dwarfs
with Benjy and Bubbles

Adapted by RUTH LERNER PERLE
Illustrated by JIM RAZZI

Holt, Rinehart and Winston • New York

Long ago, there lived a Queen—
Wicked and cruel and very mean!
Living with her, was young Snow White—
Kind and good and gentle and bright.

The Queen had a mirror she spoke to each day
And these are the words that she would say:

"Mirror, mirror, on the wall,
Who is fairest of us all?"

Then the mirror would look and decide
And this is what it always replied:

"Queen, you are lovely and you are grand;
You are the fairest in the land."

Bubbles smiled when she heard that,
For Bubbles, you know, was the Queen's mean cat.

Snow White was a sweet girl. The Queen
was mean. The Queen had a magic mirror.
It said, "Queen, you are the most beautiful!"

Then, one day, when Snow White was grown,
The Queen, in her throne room, all alone,
Asked the mirror her question in rhyme
But the answer she got was different this time:

"Mirror, mirror, on the wall,
Who is fairest of us all?"

The mirror saw the Queen and sighed,
And this is what it sadly replied:

"Queen, you are lovely, it still is true,
But now Snow White is fairer than you."

The Queen screamed out! Her face got red!
She called her woodsman and hissed as she said,
"Go to the forest and take Snow White!
Get rid of her in the dark of the night!"

One day, the mirror said,
"Snow White is the most beautiful."
The Queen said, "Get rid of Snow White!"

On the morning of the very next day,
The woodsman took Snow White away.
Benjy, the bunny came along
Because he feared something was wrong.
Along the path, the bunny hopped;
Then, suddenly, the woodsman stopped.
"I can't hurt you, Snow White," he said.
"So, I'll just leave you here instead."
With that, the woodsman went back home
Leaving Benjy and Snow White alone.

As Snow White stood afraid and still,
She saw a house upon a hill!

Snow White was left in the woods.
She saw a little house on the hill.

She ran to the house and opened the door
And wasn't frightened anymore.

A table inside had things to eat.
Seven plates each held a treat.
Near the wall were seven beds
With seven caps for seven heads.
Fourteen slippers in even rows
Stood heels to heels and toes to toes.

Benjy and Snow White tried each chair
And skipped about without a care.
They slipped on the slippers and jumped on each bed;
They ran to the table and tasted the bread.
They ate the meat from every plate,
Then went to sleep when it was late.

Snow White looked around the house.
She ate and went to sleep.

Snow White and Benjy were sleeping tight
When seven dwarfs came home in the night.
Singing a song, they tramped on the floor
But stopped in their tracks when they opened the door.
Their slippers were messed, their table askew!
A stranger had been there! The question was, "Who?"

They looked on the cupboard, the roof and each chair,
They looked up the chimney, but no one was there.
Then one of the dwarfs came running and said,
"A girl and a rabbit are asleep in my bed!"

Seven dwarfs came home.
They saw Snow White.

Snow White woke up and Benjy did too,
And the dwarfs said, "Tell us what happened to you."
They told of the Queen and the woodsman and how
They wondered what would become of them now.

"Stay with us!" all seven dwarfs cried.
"Our little house is a fine place to hide.
But always remember that you are in danger
And that *you must never speak to a stranger!*"

The dwarfs said, "Stay with us.
We will hide you."

Back at the palace, the Queen in her hall,
Asked the mirror, "Who's fairest of all?"
Bubbles, the cat, stood by her side
And listened as the mirror replied:

"Queen, you are lovely, it is true,
But there is one still fairer than you.
Deep in the woods, in a house on a hill
Lives Snow White who is lovelier still."

"Just wait!" screeched the Queen, "I'm not defeated!
I'll poison an apple and make Snow White eat it!"

The Queen then ran to take a look
In her poison fruit cookbook.
Bubbles purred as the Queen read
What the recipe for apples said:

"Stir the poison for a minute;
Drop a nice big apple in it.
When the poison starts to bubble,
You can cause a lot of trouble!"

The Queen made a poison apple.

The Queen dressed in clothes of a friendly old peasant
And painted her face to look smiling and pleasant.
She hid the bad apple in a basket of wares
With haircombs and laces and small yellow pears.

Taking the basket, she went on her way,
Reciting the sweet words that she would say.

The Queen wore an old dress. She painted
her face. She took the poison apple to
Snow White.

When the Queen arrived at the seven dwarfs' home,
She took out the apple, a lace and a comb.
"Pretty things for sale!" she cried,
"Come and see them! Step outside!"

Snow White looked out and the old woman said,
"Taste this apple! It's juicy and red."
"You'd better not!" warned Benjy, the bunny.
"If you ask me, that lady looks funny!"
The old woman smiled, "Don't let him alarm you,
How can eating an apple harm you?"
Then Snow White said, "I guess you're right,
Perhaps I'll take a tiny bite."

As soon as Snow White had a taste,
The evil Queen ran off in haste.

Snow White took the poison apple.
She took a bite.

Benjy watched as Snow White fell
And knew this was an evil spell.
He called the dwarfs, and when they came
They said the apple was to blame.

They made Snow White a bed of glass
And set it on a plot of grass
And cried for her by day and night
And never left her out of sight.

Snow White fell down.
She looked dead.

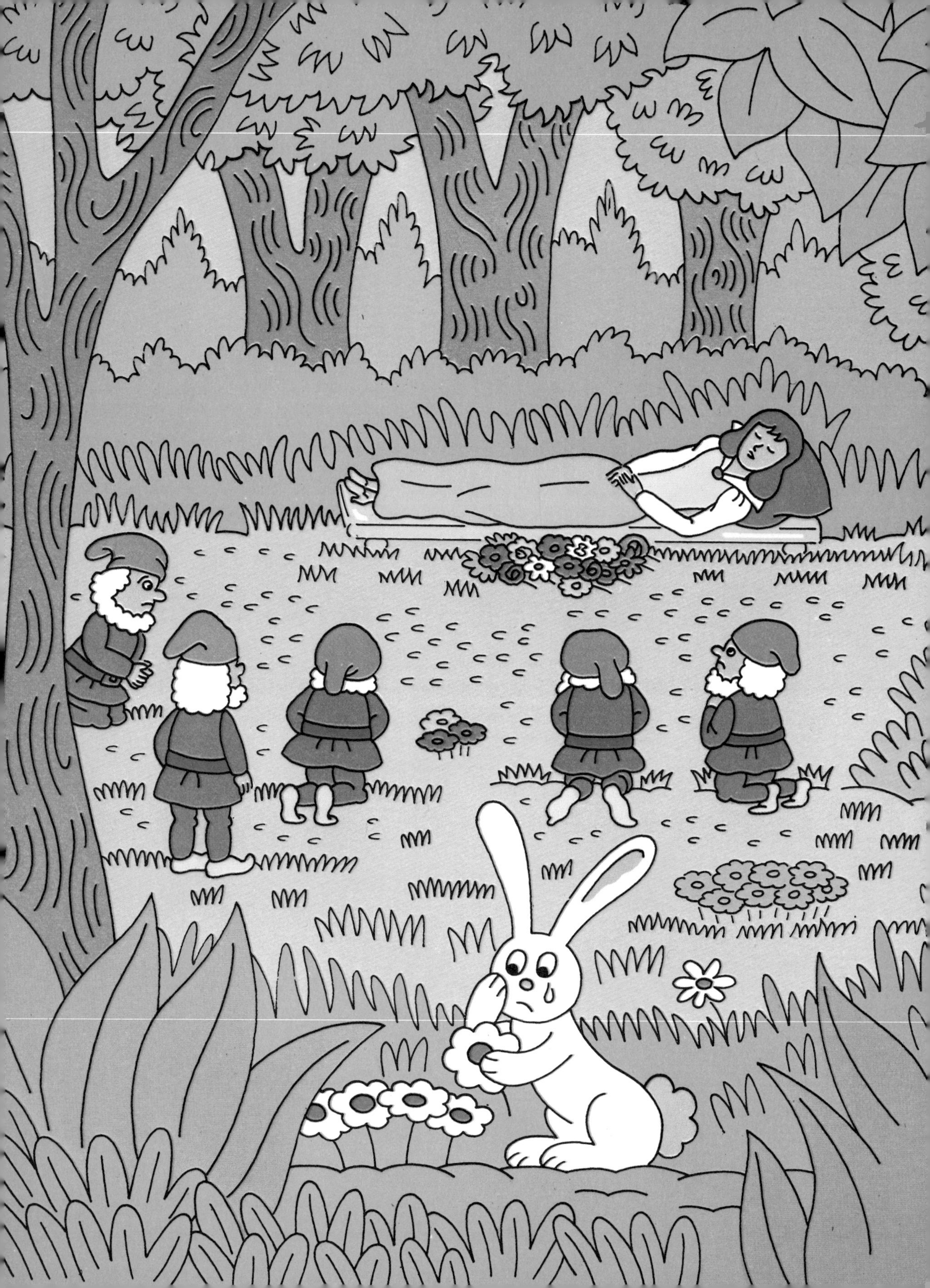

The dwarfs watched over Snow White.

Four seasons passed; the dwarfs still wept
And guarded Snow White as she slept.

Then, one day, a Prince rode by
And heard the sound of voices cry.
He saw the dwarfs with Snow White there
And asked, "Who is she, and from where?"
The dwarfs told all about Snow White
And how they watched her day and night.

The Prince was struck by Snow White's beauty
And knew at once what was his duty.
I'll take Snow White to my estate
And have my soldiers guard the gate.
With love and patience I will wait
The outcome of young Snow White's fate."

The dwarfs agreed to let him take her
Hoping that the Prince could wake her.

A Prince said, "Let me take Snow White
to my palace." The dwarfs agreed.

The Prince then called his trusty men
Who lifted Snow White up and then.
Benjy, the bunny, came hippety-hopping
His whiskers a'quiver, his long ears a'flopping!
Looking at Benjy, one trusty man tripped
And jolted Snow White as he tumbled and slipped!
The jolting and tumbling, the trip and the slip
Made the bad apple fall from her lip.

The apple was out and quick as a wink
Snow White's pale face turned lively and pink.
She sat up in wonder and looked all around her
And the Prince told her how he had found her.

The apple fell out of Snow White's mouth!
She was fine!
Then she saw the Prince.

Then the Prince said, "Snow White, be my wife.
I'll be a good husband the rest of my life."
When Snow White agreed, he gave her a ring
And said, "Soon you'll be Queen and I will be King."

All of the people came to the court;
The tall and the skinny, the stout and the short,
The braided, the curled, and those with no hair—
They were invited and they were all there!
The bunny and each of the dwarfs was a guest;
They laughed and they sang and they clapped with the rest.
The clowns and the jesters were joyful and clever!
And Snow White and the Prince…they were happy forever!

Oh, yes…
The wicked Queen danced, that wedding night
In shoes so pointy, hot and tight,
She danced herself into the ground
And by next day could not be found!
(Nor was Bubbles, the cat, around!)

Snow White married the Prince.
They were happy.

THE END